James Norrington reported that Sparrow confronted Barbossa on _Isla de Muerta_. The specifics of what happened at the island remain a mystery, but it is assumed that Sparrow killed Barbossa and became captain of the _Pearl_ once again. The cursed pirates have ceased to sail the waters, and Barbossa has not been sighted for many a night.

Elizabeth Swann has proven to be quite the enemy of the East India Trading Company. She was engaged to wed Commodore Norrington, but under the influence of Sparrow's wily and uncivilized ways, she fell in love with William Turner and decided to marry him instead. Norrington suffered greatly from the betrayal of his fiancée and was dismissed from the employ of the Royal Navy after failing to capture Sparrow.

Another point of interest pertains to the retrieval of an item belonging to Captain Sparrow. Lord Cutler Beckett, on orders from the Company, negotiated with Turner to find and return Sparrow's Compass. It is said that this is a special Compass that points not north, but to your heart's desire. Turner has yet to acquire the item.

Of further note, it has been discovered that Will Turner's father, "Bootstrap Bill" Turner, had once been a pirate on the _Black Pearl_. But Bootstrap is now trapped on the _Flying Dutchman_, doomed to serve Davy Jones forever. According to sources, it was Bootstrap who told Sparrow of Jones's intention to send his sea beast, the Kraken, after him. And it was this news that sent Sparrow to _Isla Cruces_ where Jones's heart was buried.

(To have the heart is to control Jones.) James Norrington later procured the heart on <u>Isla Cruces</u>, and for his valiant behavior he has been reinstated in the Royal Navy and promoted to admiral.

Without the heart to protect him, Sparrow was at the mercy of the Kraken. Reports claim that as he tried to flee, he was stopped by Elizabeth Swann. She chained him to the mast of the <u>Black Pearl</u> right before the Kraken surfaced and swallowed the ship . . . and Sparrow along with it.

Last our sources heard, Turner, Swann, and the <u>Pearl</u>'s crew had gone to see Tia Dalma, a powerful mystic who lives in a dark bayou. Rumor has it that she has brought Barbossa back from the dead to help retrieve Sparrow from Davy Jones's Locker.

It is our understanding that despite his apparent "death," Captain Jack Sparrow is still a threat. It is up to the Royal Navy and members of the East India Trading Company to determine Sparrow's status and put an official end to his pirating ways.

Regards,

Admiral Bratton

Admiral Bratton
of the HMS <u>Century</u>

THE MOVIE STORYBOOK

Printed in the United States of America

First Edition

3 5 7 9 10 8 6 4 2

This book is set in Romic Light 14 pt.

Library of Congress Catalog Card Number: 2006909023

ISBN-13: 978 1-4231-0378-3
ISBN-10: 1-4231-0378-5

DisneyPirates.Com

DISNEP

PIRATES of the CARIBBEAN

AT WORLD'S END

THE MOVIE STORYBOOK

Adapted by T.T. Sutherland
Based on the screenplay written by Ted Elliott & Terry Rossio
Based on characters created by Ted Elliott & Terry Rossio
and Stuart Beattie and Jay Wolpert
Based on Walt Disney's Pirates of the Caribbean
Produced by Jerry Bruckheimer
Directed by Gore Verbinski

DISNEP PRESS
New York

A pirate song echoed softly through the dark alleys and waterways of Singapore's busy harbor. It came from a slim figure tying a boat to a dock. Hearing the song, a menacing pirate stepped out of the darkness and approached the new arrival. The man's name was Tai Huang, and he was the chief lieutenant of Singapore's Pirate Lord, Captain Sao Feng.

"A dangerous song to be singing," Huang said. The figure looked up. It was Elizabeth Swann. Tai Huang continued, "particularly for a woman alone."

"What makes you think she's alone?" said a new voice.

Tai Huang turned to find the pirate Barbossa standing behind him.

"Your master is expecting us," Barbossa said.

Meanwhile, something was moving in the water below the docks. It looked like a bunch of coconuts floating by . . . but under each coconut hid a member of the crew of the notorious pirate, Captain Jack Sparrow. Following along with the first mate, Gibbs, came Marty, Pintel, Ragetti, and Cotton. As quietly as they could, they swam up to a metal grate. Above them, agents from the East India Trading Company stood, their eyes scanning the harbor for signs of trouble.

Squeak, squeak, squeak. Jack's crew began to file through the metal. Hearing the noise, the guards looked up but all they saw was an old woman, pushing a cart full of birdcages. They did not know that the old woman was actually Tia Dalma, a powerful mystic.

The noise of Tia Dalma's cart masked the sound of Jack's crew as they filed through the grate. Finally they broke through, and one by one, they slipped into the tunnels leading under Sao Feng's hideout—a bathhouse. It was filled with nasty pipes, algae-covered tubs, and lots of steam. The crew waited.

Elizabeth and Barbossa arrived at the bathhouse and were ordered to disarm. Elizabeth noticed that all the pirates had the same dragon tattoo—Sao Feng's symbol. Finally, Sao Feng himself stepped forward.

Barbossa explained that he was in need of a ship and a crew. Sao Feng chuckled. "That's an odd coincidence," he said. "Earlier this day, a thief broke into my most revered uncle's temple and tried to make off with these." He held up navigational charts showing the route to

World's End—beyond which lay Davy Jones's Locker . . . and Jack Sparrow.

Sao Feng gestured, and his guards dragged the thief forward.

It was Will Turner, Elizabeth's fiancé.

When Sao Feng drew his knife to kill him, Elizabeth tensed. Now Sao Feng knew the three were working together.

"You come into my city," he snarled, "and you betray me?"

"No," Barbossa said. Then he revealed that a meeting of the
Brethren Court had been called. The Brethren Court was made up of
nine Pirate Lords. Many generations ago, another group of Lords had
come together to establish control over the sea. To do so, they had
captured the sea goddess, Calypso, and imprisoned her in human
form so she could no longer send storms to destroy them. They had

also created the Pirate Code to bring order. Ever since then, pirates had ruled the seas.

But now that rule was being challenged. The East India Trading Company, under the control of Lord Cutler Beckett, was wiping out pirates all across the Caribbean and the world. The only way to stop Beckett was for the pirates to unite and fight him.

Sao Feng had one more question. He wanted to know why they needed the maps to the next world. "What is it you seek in Davy Jones's Locker?" he asked.

"Jack Sparrow," Will answered.

Sao Feng's face darkened. "The only reason I would want Jack Sparrow returned from the realm of the dead is so I can send him back myself."

But there was a good reason to bring Jack Sparrow back, Barbossa explained. Jack was a Pirate Lord, which meant that he had one of the nine Pieces of Eight. Every Pirate Lord was supposed to pass along his Piece of Eight before he died, but Jack had failed to do so. The only way to get it back so they could convene the Court was to go to Davy Jones's Locker, find Jack, and bring him back.

As Barbossa spoke, Sao Feng spotted something. In the steam, the dragon tattoo on one of his men was melting. It was a fake! Will was not the only traitor among them! Sao Feng ordered his guards to seize the man named Steng.

The pirates hiding in the steam tunnels below heard the commotion and knew this meant trouble. Quickly, they passed swords up through the floorboards to Barbossa, Elizabeth, and Will. Within seconds, everyone's sword was drawn. Sao Feng's pointed at Steng. "Drop your weapons, or I kill your man!" Sao Feng snarled.

Barbossa and Elizabeth exchanged glances. They had never seen Steng before. Barbossa shrugged. "Kill him. He's not our man."

"If he's not with you, and not us . . ." Will said, "who *is* he with?"

CRASH! The answer came smashing through the windows. East India Trading Company agents stormed into the room. The pirates turned to fight them. Swords clashed, and explosions rocked the bathhouse. Pirates scattered into the streets.

One of the agents was Beckett's clerk, Mr. Mercer. Mercer had had a run-in with Elizabeth and Will before and knew to keep an extra close eye on them. Glancing around, he spied Sao Feng talking to Will in a shadowy corner. He crept up on them with his pistol drawn. But just as he was about to shoot . . . he heard something that made him pause.

"You want to cut a deal with Beckett?" Will said to Sao Feng. "You need what I offer." Sao Feng nodded and handed over the charts.

As Mercer continued to watch, Barbossa and Elizabeth ran over to Will. He had the charts *and* a ship. Together they escaped on the ship, a Chinese junk called the *Hai Peng*, along with Tai Huang and a full crew. Before they left, Mercer overheard Will say they would meet Sao Feng at Shipwreck Cove. He smiled. Lord Beckett would be very interested to hear about all this.

A while later and half a world away, Mercer stood on the deck of the HMS *Endeavour* with Admiral James Norrington, Elizabeth's father, Governor Swann, and Lord Beckett. Moments before, the *Flying Dutchman*, under Beckett's orders, had attacked a group of pirate ships.

The *Endeavour* came up alongside the *Dutchman*, and Beckett and Swann followed Norrington aboard Davy Jones's ship. With them was the Dead Man's Chest, and inside was the still-beating heart of Davy Jones. Having the heart gave Lord Beckett control over the *Flying Dutchman*. Jones knew that Beckett could stab the heart and kill him at any moment. This was why he was now attacking pirates and following orders from the East India Trading Company. Beckett had even ordered Jones to destroy his pet leviathan, the Kraken—the very monster that had killed Jack Sparrow—and Jones had done it.

Governor Swann was not happy to see the carnage the *Dutchman* had left. "Did you give those ships an opportunity to surrender?" he demanded. "My daughter could have been aboard one of them!"

"I am exterminating pirates—as commanded by the Company," Davy Jones sneered. "And your daughter is dead, pulled under with the *Black Pearl* by my pet. Did Lord Beckett not tell you that?"

The governor was heartbroken. He ran to the captain's cabin,

where Norrington was standing guard over the chest. When the admiral heard that Elizabeth was dead, his face grew pale. Before he could act, Swann snatched up a bayonet to stab the heart. But just then, Davy Jones entered the cabin, followed by Beckett.

"No!" Jones yelled. "If you slay the heart, then yours must take its place—and you must take mine," Jones said. "The *Dutchman* must always have a captain."

Swann faltered. He did not want to end up like Davy Jones, doomed to follow Beckett's orders and unable to touch land but once every ten years. Norrington grabbed the weapon away from Swann and escorted him out of the cabin.

"I can order Admiral Norrington's silence," Lord Beckett said as he closed the chest that held the heart. "He'll obey; it's what he does."

Mercer had entered the room as well. Now he stepped forward and asked, "And the governor?"

"Yes. Well. Every man should have a secret."

Meanwhile, the *Hai Peng* was sailing through icy waters. Will shivered and leaned over Sao Feng's charts. He couldn't make any sense of them. He read one of the inscribed poems out loud: *"Over the edge, back, over again, sunrise sets, flash of green."* What could it possibly mean?

"Do not fret, Mister Turner," said Barbossa. "We will find the way. It's not getting to the Land of the Dead that's the problem—it's getting back!"

All of a sudden, a roaring sound filled the air. It seemed to be getting closer and closer. But Barbossa did not appear worried. "Aye, these be the waters I know," he said. "You have to be lost, to find a place as can't be found."

Tia Dalma came on deck and looked around. She knew Jack was not far now. She cast a set of crab claws onto a barrel and murmured an incantation.

Will couldn't believe it. They were heading directly toward a giant waterfall, where the ocean dropped down and down and down . . . into nothingness. But no one was trying to stop the ship.

The roaring waterfall dragged them closer and closer, until finally they plummeted over World's End and down into the darkness.

Captain Jack Sparrow strode onto the deck of the *Black Pearl*. A sail was flapping loose in the wind. He made it fast and called up: "Haul the halyard, slacken braces!"

But the sails were still. The ship was not moving. There was no one else on deck. Jack Sparrow was alone and talking to himself in Davy Jones's Locker.

And to make matters worse, the *Black Pearl* was sitting in the middle of a vast desert.

Jack slid down to the desert floor and picked up a line tied to the *Pearl*. With a heave, he tried to pull his ship along behind him. He put all his weight into it, but it was no use. The *Pearl* didn't move.

Jack slumped down into the sand. "No wind," he muttered. He sat with his head bowed for a long time.

Suddenly he saw a shadow rising above him. He looked up.

The *Black Pearl* was moving! The ship was sailing along the desert floor!

He looked under the ship and saw thousands of chittering crabs. They had lifted the ship onto their backs and were carrying it along.

At last, Captain Jack Sparrow and the *Pearl* were on the move again!

Not far away, the crew of the *Hai Peng* had just washed up on the shoreline of the desert. Their ship was a wreck, and everyone was in tatters. Will was furious.

"We are trapped here, by your doing," Will said to Barbossa. "No different than Jack."

"Witty Jack be closer than you think," Tia Dalma said.

Puzzled by the mystic's words, Will and Elizabeth looked toward the distant skyline. She was right! The *Black Pearl* was sailing over the desert floor—straight toward them.

The ship splashed down in the water, and Jack jumped out.

"Will! Gibbs!" Jack shouted. "Were you killed by the Kraken?"

Ignoring his mean-spirited comment, Elizabeth ran up to Jack and hugged him tightly. "I'm so sorry," she said, referring to the fact that she had sent him to the Locker. "So glad you're all right."

One by one, Jack took in his saviors. But then a voice spoke up, and he froze.

"How ye be, Jack Sparrow?" said the voice. Jack turned and saw Barbossa.

Barbossa was supposed to be dead. Jack had killed him himself. So Jack was a little more than surprised to see him.

"Barbossa!" cried Jack. "You old scoundrel! I haven't seen you in too long. Not since . . ."

"*Isla de Muerta*, remember? You shot me!" Barbossa opened his shirt to show the scar. "Right here! Lodged in my heart, it did."

"I remember," Jack said. "I wouldn't forget that!"

"We came to rescue you," Barbossa explained.

Jack thought for a moment. "Did you now?" he said. "How kind. But it would seem as I possess a ship, and you don't, *you're* the ones in need of rescuing."

Barbossa pointed at the *Black Pearl*. "I see my ship right there."

Each man believed that he was the captain of the *Pearl*, and they started to argue. Will jumped in to stop them. He told Jack that Lord Beckett was using the *Dutchman* to take over the Seven Seas. Then Tia Dalma pointed out that Jack *had* to come back with them. The Brethren Court had been called.

"Why should I sail with any of you?" Jack asked. "Four of you have tried to kill me." He looked at Elizabeth. "One of you succeeded."

Finally, Jack agreed to let them all join him on the *Pearl*. He took out his Compass to see where they should go. The needle was spinning like crazy.

"Ja-ack," Barbossa said. He held up the charts and waved them. "Which way are you going, Jack?"

Time passed slowly. There was no more water to drink. The *Pearl* was drifting on a quiet sea, and night was coming.

"If we cannot escape these doldrums before night, I fear we sail on . . . forever," Tia Dalma said ominously.

Jack did not like the sound of that. He studied Sao Feng's charts. He lined up some of the Chinese characters and realized they read: UP IS DOWN.

Suddenly he had an idea. "Not sun-set. Sun-down. And rise—up!" He stood and pointed. "Over there! What's that?" He ran to the side of the ship. All the pirates chased after him, and the ship tilted to one side. Then Jack ran back to starboard. "There, it moved!" He ran back to port again.

The ship rocked from side to side as everyone ran after him. Barbossa came on deck and noticed the sun setting. He realized what Jack was doing. He was trying to flip the *Pearl* over!

"Aye, he's onto it!" Barbossa yelled. "All hands together!"

The ship tipped farther and farther over. The sun sank lower in the sky. Then, just as the sun disappeared into the sea, Jack yelled: "And now up is down!" and the ship overturned completely.

Everyone was underwater. Things began to float away.

On the horizon, there was a flash of green!

And suddenly . . . *THWUMP!*

All of the water fell away with a giant splash. Everything that had been floating off fell back onto the deck.

The *Black Pearl* was floating right side up on a calm sea at sunrise. They were back in the real world!

When everyone had calmed down, Will suggested sailing to the nearest island for water.

But when they arrived, Jack and Barbossa couldn't agree on who got to stay with the ship. So they both headed for shore while Will stayed with the *Pearl*.

Moments later, the pirates came across a dead body in a freshwater spring. It was Steng—the agent who had attacked Sao Feng in Singapore. That didn't seem right. They rushed back to the beach to find Tai Huang holding a pistol aimed at them. Behind him stood his crew. Out by the reef, the Chinese fighting ship, the *Empress*, was floating beside the *Black Pearl*. What was going on?

The Chinese pirates hustled the landing party back onto the deck of the *Pearl,* where two guards held Elizabeth. Sao Feng was also standing there, smiling. He stepped over to Jack. "Jack Sparrow. You paid me a great insult, once." Then he punched Jack in the jaw.

Will came onto the deck and saw Elizabeth in chains. "She's not part of the bargain," he said to Sao Feng. "Release her."

"And what bargain be that?" Barbossa asked.

"You heard Captain Turner," Sao Feng said to his guards. "Release her."

"*Captain* Turner?" Jack cried.

"Aye, the perfidious rotter led a mutiny against us," said Gibbs.

Jack sighed. "It's always the quiet ones."

"Why didn't you tell me you were planning this?" Elizabeth asked Will when she had been released.

"It was my burden to bear," he said. "I need the *Pearl*. That's the only reason I came on this voyage."

Jack looked around at his crew. Had anyone come to save him just because they missed him?

Sao Feng grabbed Jack's arm. "I'm sorry, Jack, but there's an old friend who wants to see you." He nodded over Jack's shoulder.

The *Endeavour* was coming around the island.

Jack was taken to the captain's cabin of the *Endeavour*, where Lord Beckett stood at a window, gazing out to sea. Jack's things were dumped on the table, including his Compass.

Jack asked what Beckett wanted. Beckett held up the Compass.

"You've brought me this. I owe you a pardon and a commission. So I am offering you a job. In the employ of the East India Trading Company. Working for me."

Jack refused Beckett's offer proudly. "We've been down that road before, haven't we?" he said.

"I had contracted you to deliver cargo on my behalf," Beckett said. "You chose to liberate it."

"People aren't cargo, mate," Jack said.

"You haven't changed," Beckett sniffed. "Our business is concluded. Enjoy the gallows."

But Jack had a counterproposal. If Beckett made Jones cancel Jack's debt and let Jack go free, Jack would lead Beckett straight to Shipwreck Cove where the Brethren Court was meeting . . . and where all the powerful Pirate Lords would be.

Back on the deck of the *Pearl*, Sao Feng's men took Will by surprise and shackled his arms. Then Sao Feng turned to Mercer.

"Beckett agreed, the *Black Pearl* was to be mine," Sao Feng said.

Mercer smiled. "Lord Beckett wouldn't give up the one ship as might prove a match for the *Dutchman*, would he?"

Sao Feng looked around. His men were outnumbered. He sighed and let one of Mercer's men take the wheel.

Sao Feng was convinced that the East India Trading Company would win. There was no point in trying to fight. "They have the *Dutchman*," Sao Feng said, moving closer to Barbossa. "And what do the Brethren have?"

"We have . . . Calypso," Barbossa said.

Sao Feng was shocked. He glanced at Elizabeth, standing across the deck. "Calypso," he murmured. "An old legend."

"No," Barbossa said, drawing Sao Feng's attention away from Elizabeth. "The goddess herself, bound in human form."

Sao Feng agreed to help them escape Beckett's men, on one condition. He wanted Elizabeth.

Barbossa said no, but Elizabeth overheard and interjected. "Done," she said. Horrified, Will tried to stop her.

"My choice," Elizabeth insisted.

"Then we have an accord?" Barbossa asked.

"Agreed," said Sao Feng.

Back aboard the *Endeavour*, Jack and Beckett's negotiation was interrupted by the explosion of cannon fire. Jack grabbed his Compass from the table and followed Beckett up on deck.

The *Empress* was sailing away! And on the *Black Pearl*, Barbossa, Will, and Sao Feng's men had overpowered Beckett's and were throwing them overboard. Quickly, Jack looked for a way to get to his ship. He seized a cannon and pointed it toward the *Black Pearl*.

"You're mad," Beckett said.

"Thank goodness for that," replied Jack. "Because if I weren't, this would never work." Then he jumped on top and set the cannon off. The cannonball smashed through the railing and flew through the air toward the *Pearl*, where Jack landed unharmed.

"Tell me you didn't miss me!" he said to Barbossa. He ordered Will to be taken to the brig. The *Pearl* had its captain back and was on its way to Shipwreck Cove.

Beckett couldn't chase them right away. Jack's cannon blast had not only broken the railing, but one of the masts as well. They would have to fix it first. But that didn't mean the *Dutchman* couldn't give chase. . . .

The captain's cabin on the *Empress* was hung with silk and covered in luxurious pillows. Elizabeth stood in the middle of it, dressed in a beautiful Chinese gown. Sao Feng entered and offered her a drink.

"I admit, this is not how I expected to be treated," Elizabeth said warily.

"No other treatment would be worthy of you . . . Calypso," answered Sao Feng.

Elizabeth didn't know what to say.

Just then, a massive explosion rocked the ship. Cannonballs

slammed into the hull. Elizabeth looked out and saw a ship attacking them. It was the *Flying Dutchman*!

When she turned back, she found Sao Feng lying on the floor, badly wounded.

"Here, please," he murmured. He took off the rope-knot pendant he always wore. "The Captain's Knot. Take it. Take it!"

"*Me?*" Elizabeth asked.

"Go in my place to Shipwreck Cove," Sao Feng instructed.

Tai Huang burst into the room.

Elizabeth held up the pendant. "He made me captain."

Meanwhile Norrington led the crew of the *Flying Dutchman* aboard the *Empress*. "I heard you were dead," Norrington said when he saw Elizabeth. He was even more shocked to find out that she was not only alive, she was now captain of the *Empress*.

Norrington had no choice. He ordered Elizabeth and her crew to the *Dutchman*'s brig.

As she was being locked in her cell, Elizabeth remembered that Will's father was aboard the *Dutchman*. She called to one of the crewmen.

"Bootstrap?" she tried. "Bill Turner?"

Eyes opened in the hull beside her.

"You know my name," croaked the face in the wall. It was Will's father!

"I know your son," Elizabeth said.

But Bootstrap barely remembered that Will had promised to save him. His memory was fading; most of him had become part of the ship.

With the *Endeavour*'s mast finally fixed, Beckett chased after the *Black Pearl*. In the distance, he spied a flock of gulls. As the birds got closer, he saw that they were circling a dead body in the water. It was one of his own men. The body had been tied to a barrel so it would float. Attached to him was a bottle with a note bearing the symbol of the East India Trading Company. Beckett looked up and saw another flock of gulls in the distance.

Someone was leaving a trail for him to follow.

Later that night, on board the *Pearl*, that someone was lashing another body to a barrel. It was Will Turner. Hearing a sound on the deck behind him, he whirled around.

"I knew the brig wouldn't hold you," said Jack.

Will drew his sword, but Jack just looked down at the body beside Will.

"What do you intend to do, once you've given up the location of the Brethren?" Jack asked, figuring out Will's plan.

"Ask Beckett to free my father," Will answered.

Jack scoffed. He knew Lord Beckett wouldn't keep that bargain. The cost of killing Davy Jones was too high.

Suddenly, Jack had an idea. What if *he* killed Davy Jones? That way, Bootstrap would still be freed, plus Jack would be immortal. "I get aboard the *Dutchman*, I find the chest, I stab the beating thing," Jack told Will. "Your father goes free from his debt, you are free to be with your charming murderess, and I am free to sail the seas forever."

Jack handed Will his Compass and shoved him into the water. The body tied to the barrel splashed down beside him. Will clung to the barrel. Above him, Jack smiled and waved as the *Pearl* sailed away.

"I hate him," Will said.

In another part of the ocean, the *Dutchman* was towing the *Empress* through the dark water.

Elizabeth looked up as her jail door opened. Admiral Norrington was standing there. He had decided to free Elizabeth.

Elizabeth and her crew followed Norrington up to the towline. One by one, they started crawling across the rope to the *Empress*.

"Do not go to Shipwreck Cove," Norrington said to Elizabeth. He told her there was a traitor among the Brethren and that Beckett knew all about the meeting.

Elizabeth would not change her mind. "Come with us," she said instead.

Suddenly a noise came out of the darkness.

Norrington turned and drew his sword. "Go!" he said to Elizabeth.

She turned and ran across to the safety of the *Empress*.

Meanwhile, Jack was on his way to the gathering of the Brethren Court.

Shipwreck Island was hollow, with a round water cove inside it. Only pirates knew how to find the way inside.

The *Black Pearl* sailed through the hidden passage into the cove, and the crew got their first glimpse of Shipwreck City. The city was made of the ruins of broken, derelict ships, floating together in the center of the cove. Pirate ships from across the world were moored around it.

"Look at them all!" one of the crew murmured.

"There's not been a gathering like this in our lifetime," Barbossa said.

Jack sighed. "And I owe all of them money."

The chamber of the Brethren Court was located in the abandoned hull of a ship. To one side stood a globe with eight swords stabbed into it, each belonging to a Pirate Lord. All but one of the Lords had arrived and were now seated at the center table. The rest of the chamber was packed with ordinary pirates.

From his spot among the Lords, Barbossa hammered on the table with a cannonball. He demanded that the Pirate Lords each throw their Piece of Eight into the wooden bowl on the table. One by one they did so, starting with Ammand the Corsair. Next came Villanueva, a Spaniard, followed by Captain Chevalle, an aristocratic Frenchman. The next Pirate Lord was Gentleman Jocard, a pirate who had once been a slave, and the next was Mistress Ching, a Chinese pirate. Then there was Sri Sumbhajee, a serene pirate from India, who was flanked by two big guards. Finally, there were Barbossa and Jack.

"We're still short one Pirate Lord," Jack said. "I'm content to wait until Sao Feng joins us."

Suddenly the sound of footsteps filled the room. Everyone turned to see Elizabeth, who had arrived with Tai Huang and was to take Sao Feng's place.

Tai Huang indicated the globe and Elizabeth stabbed her sword into it. "Listen!" she announced. "Our location has been betrayed! Jones—under the command of Lord Beckett—is on his way here!"

"And who is this betrayer?" asked Gentleman Jocard.

"It does not matter how they found us!" Barbossa continued. "The question is, what will we do now that they have?"

"We fight," said Elizabeth.

A short while later, ships gathered outside the island, ready for battle. On every deck, pirates sharpened their swords, waiting.

All at once, the *Endeavour* sailed into view. The pirates let out bloodcurdling yells of excitement . . . but slowly their shouts faded as another ship sailed into view . . . and another . . . and another.

The whole East India Trading Company had arrived!

Then the *Flying Dutchman* rose out of the water ahead of the ships, ready to lead the enormous fleet.

"Parlay?" Jack suggested.

On opposite ends of a sparkling white sandbar, two longboats were beached. From one end of the sandbar came Jack, Elizabeth, and Barbossa. From the other came Davy Jones, Will, and Lord Beckett.

"You be the cur that led these wolves to our door," Barbossa said to Will accusingly.

Elizabeth's face grew pale as Beckett laughed. Will was just a tool, he pointed out. Jack was the real architect of the betrayal.

Jack denied the whole thing, and Will agreed. Will had his own mission to fulfill.

"If Turner was not acting on your behalf, then how did he come to give me this?" Beckett asked, holding up Jack's Compass. Now Barbossa believed it—Jack really had betrayed them. But why?

Davy Jones still demanded that Jack's debt be paid. One hundred years of servitude aboard the *Dutchman* . . . as a start.

"There's no better end for Jack Sparrow than bilge rat aboard the *Flying Dutchman*," Elizabeth said. "I propose an exchange. Will leaves with us . . . and you can have Jack."

"Done," said Will.

"Not done," protested Jack.

"Done," said Beckett, smugly.

Elizabeth had had enough. "We will fight," she said to Beckett, "and surely you will die."

The Parlay was over. Jack was dragged away to the brig of the *Flying Dutchman*. The others returned to the *Pearl*. The battle for control of the Seven Seas was about to begin.

Back aboard the *Pearl*, Elizabeth climbed onto the rail of the ship and rallied the crew. "Listen to me!" she yelled. "The Brethren will still be looking here, to us, to the *Black Pearl*, to lead. What will they see? They will see free men. And freedom!" She met their eyes.

Jack may have betrayed them all, and Will might have hurt her, but she was a Pirate Lord now. And she would not let Beckett's men win. Together, the pirates could battle back. They had done it before. The East India Trading Company would *never* rule the seas.

"Hoist the colors!" she yelled as loudly as she could. "Because today, we are the **Pirates of the Caribbean!**"